FRIGHTVILLE

NIGHT OF THE MASK

FRIGHTVILLE

NIGHT OF THE MASK

BY MIKE FORD

Scholastic Inc.

Special thanks to Donna Lowich

ISBN 978-1-338-36015-8

10 9 8 7 6 5 4 3 2 1   20 21 22 23 24

Printed in the U.S.A.   40
First printing 2020

Book design by Stephanie Yang

FOR ERIK

Tucker opened the small gold envelope that had his name written across the front in perfectly printed letters, and removed the pink card from inside. Instead of having ordinary writing on it, it was engraved like a fancy invitation.

COME CELEBRATE SASHA'S BIRTHDAY! it said.

"It's Saturday," said Sasha, who just moments ago had handed Tucker the envelope and was still standing in front of him, smiling widely.

Before Tucker could even read the rest of the card, she continued. "It starts at two o'clock. You don't *have* to bring a present, but I won't be mad if you do. Oh, and it's a costume party. Well, sort of. Everyone is going to wear masks. I thought that would be fun."

"What kind of masks?" Tucker asked.

"Any kind really," said Sasha. "Superheroes. Animals. Monsters. Whatever you want. And don't worry about being able to get around in your chair. The hallways are super wide, there are ramps to the doors, and there's even an elevator that goes between floors. You'll have no problem."

"Cool," Tucker said. He tried to sound like it was no big deal, but going to Sasha's house was actually a *huge* deal. She didn't just live in a house—she lived in a mansion. It sat on a hill overlooking the town, and had a long driveway that circled the hill five times before reaching the top. The mansion was very old, with lots of pointed roofs, and seven chimneys, and probably hundreds of windows. It even had a name— Stormwatch House. Tucker had always wanted to see the inside of it. Now he was going to.

"So, you'll come?" Sasha asked.

"Definitely," said Tucker.

Sasha grinned and bounced on her toes. "Yay," she said. "Okay, I've got to hand out the rest of these invitations. I'll see you later."

She darted off. Tucker looked at the invitation again, thinking about what kind of mask he might want to wear. There were so many possibilities. As he was considering them, his mother pulled up in their minivan. The side door slid open, and the ramp extended. Tucker expertly maneuvered his electric chair up it and into the van.

"How was your day?" his mother asked as the ramp retracted and the door slid shut.

"Great," Tucker said. "I got a ninety-three on my science test, and my audition for the musical went really well. I'm pretty sure I'm going to be either the Tin Man or the Cowardly Lion."

"That sounds like a pretty great day," his mother said as she pulled out of the school parking lot.

"Maybe that's what I should be for the party," Tucker said, thinking out loud. "A lion."

"What party?" his mother asked.

Tucker told her about Sasha's birthday party.

"You're going to get to see the inside of Stormwatch House?" his mother said. "Maybe I should call Sasha's mother and volunteer to help.

I'm dying to see the inside of that house. It would be the perfect setting for this idea I have."

Tucker groaned. His mother wrote horror novels, and she was always having ideas. So far, she'd published four books. She wasn't as famous as some other writers, but her books were great. At least, Tucker assumed they were. He hadn't actually read any of them, because he didn't like to be scared. But lots of people had told them how good they were.

"This party isn't for you!" he objected.

His mother laughed. "Okay," she said. "But I want you to take notes on how the rooms look."

"Mom!" Tucker said, making a face at her in the rearview mirror.

"I'm joking," his mother said. "Well, mostly."

"Anyway, I need to get a mask," Tucker said,

hoping to distract her. "It's kind of a costume party."

"I know just the place," his mother said. "I saw a new store the other day when I drove to the cemetery to get ideas for character names from the old gravestones. It's called Frightville."

"Frightville?" Tucker said. "That sounds—"

"Scary," his mother interrupted. "I know. That's why I want to check it out. It looks like some kind of antique shop or something. I bet they'll have masks."

Tucker started to ask her why an antique store would have masks, but he knew better. His mother wanted to check out Frightville, and she was using this as her excuse. He would go along with her, and when it turned out the store didn't have anything for him, he would ask her to take him to Party World in the shopping center. Then maybe he could talk her into getting a ham and pineapple pizza at Pie in the Sky for dinner, since it was right next door.

A few minutes later, they pulled up to Frightville. Tucker wheeled himself down the van's ramp, then through the door of the store. As his mother went off to browse on her own, Tucker took a look around. His mother had kind of been right about it being an antique store, but not the sort of antiques you usually found for sale. Everything in Frightville was a little bit creepy. Instead of old tables and lamps, the store was filled with things like real stuffed crows with glinting glass eyes and cases crammed with books that had titles like *Toadstool Soup and Other Deadly Dishes*. There was even a cabinet cluttered with dusty glass bottles and a sign that read: MAY CONTAIN GENIES: OPEN AT YOUR OWN RISK.

"Good afternoon," a voice said, making Tucker jump.

A man was standing beside him. He was tall and thin, and he was dressed in a black suit. His gray hair was slicked back, and he regarded Tucker with eyes the same color as his hair. "My apologies for startling you," he said. "My name is Odson Ends. This is my store."

"Oh," Tucker said. "It's, um, really great." He looked around, hoping his mother had finished browsing and they could go, but she was nowhere to be seen.

"Is there anything I can help you find?" Mr. Ends inquired.

"I don't think so," Tucker said. "I mean, I

need a mask for this party I'm going to, but I doubt you have anything like that."

Mr. Ends smiled. It was like a crack appearing on frozen ice. "Come with me," he said.

Tucker followed along behind as Mr. Ends went down an aisle. They stopped in front of a wall on which dozens of masks dangled from wooden pegs. They weren't the usual plastic or rubber masks like the ones sold at Party World. These looked handmade.

"They're papier-mâché," Mr. Ends explained, pronouncing the last part with an accent.

Tucker knew that papier-mâché was just a fancy word meaning paper mixed with water and glue. He'd made some himself the summer before in art class at Camp Weedpatch. But he'd never seen anything like the masks on the wall. They were weird and wonderful. A few were scary, like the witch face with a long, crooked nose and the thing that looked like a sea monster. Others were more fanciful, like a big-eared rabbit and an elf.

"The magical thing about masks is that they let you turn yourself into what you want the world to see you as," Mr. Ends said. "Do you see anything here you would like to be?"

Tucker thought it was a strange way of asking if he liked any of them. He looked at all the faces staring back at him. *Who do I want to be?* he wondered. *Or what?*

He liked a lot of the masks. But which one felt the most like who he was? He considered a cat face, which was kind of like the lion from *The Wizard of Oz*, but it wasn't quite right. Neither were the clown, or the fish head, or the face made out of green leaves and flowers. He was about to say that none of them were what he was looking for. Then his eyes stopped on a mask. It was shaped like a bat, and the eyeholes were in the middle of its wings. It wasn't as unusual or fanciful as the others, but Tucker liked it.

"That one," he said, pointing.

"An interesting choice," Mr. Ends said as he took the mask from its peg and handed it to Tucker.

"What's interesting about it?" Tucker asked.

"I'm sure you've heard the expression 'blind as a bat,'" Mr. Ends said. "It's not true, of course. Bats actually see quite well. But they also use echolocation—sound waves—to navigate in the dark and find food. It's an extraordinary ability, being able to see things that would otherwise be invisible."

Tucker placed the mask over his face and looked through the eyeholes.

"Do things look any different?" Mr. Ends asked.

"I don't think so," Tucker said.

"Hmm," Mr. Ends replied. "Well, sometimes a mask is just a mask."

"Sure," Tucker agreed, although he really had no idea what the man was talking about. He removed the mask and held it in his hands. He still wasn't quite sure why he liked it so much, but somehow, he knew it was perfect for Sasha's party. He looked up at Mr. Ends. "I'll take it."

2

On Saturday, Tucker's mom and dad flipped a coin to see who would get to drive him to the party and who would stay there to wait for Tucker's great-aunt Hilda, who was due to arrive for a week's visit. To Tucker's relief, his dad won.

"She's *your* aunt," his mother said to his father as he gleefully hopped into the van. "And I'm picking you up!" she told Tucker.

Tucker couldn't blame her for being

disappointed. He was excited too. Fifteen minutes later, as they rounded the final curve of the driveway and Stormwatch House loomed over them, he stared up at it through the window in awe. "Wow," he said. "It's practically a castle."

While he was rolling his chair down the ramp, the front door of the house opened and Sasha came running out, accompanied by a short, round woman who looked like a grown-up version of Sasha. The two of them came over to the van, and the woman held out her hand to Tucker.

"I'm Aretta Okafor," she said. "Sasha's mother."

"*Dr.* Okafor," said Sasha proudly.

Her mother laughed. "Only when I'm at the hospital," she said.

"It's nice to meet you, Dr. Okafor," Tucker

said, shaking her hand. "This is my dad. He's a plumber."

"That's almost the same thing," Sasha's mother said. "We both figure out what's going on with the insides."

"Speaking of plumbing," Tucker's dad said, pointing at the house, "this place must have miles of pipes in it."

"It does," Dr. Okafor agreed. "And all of them are a hundred years old and leaking. Maybe when you have time, you can come look at them for us."

"I'd be happy to," Tucker's dad said. "Right now, I think these two have a party to get to."

Sasha glanced down at the wrapped box resting on Tucker's lap. "Is that for me?" she said. "I told you that you didn't have to bring a present." She grinned. "But I'm glad you did.

Come on, I'll show you where you can put it."

Tucker said goodbye to his dad, then followed Sasha to the door of the house. Sasha's mother followed behind them. "I'm going to go see how your father is getting on with the refreshments," she said, disappearing through a doorway and leaving Sasha and Tucker alone.

"Am I the first one here?" Tucker asked.

"There are some others," Sasha said as she started walking down a long hallway. "They're in the ballroom."

"This place has a ballroom?" said Tucker.

"It has all *kinds* of rooms," Sasha told him. "I don't think I've even seen all of them. Once, my brother and I played hide-and-seek, and I didn't find him for two days."

Tucker wasn't sure whether to believe that or not, so he turned his attention to the walls.

They were covered in paintings of all kinds. Mostly, they were modern-looking, with lots of bright blobs and streaks of color.

"My dad did these," Sasha said. "He's an artist." She stopped in front of one that was different from the rest. "Except this one. This one was here when we moved in."

The painting was a portrait. It depicted a serious, dark-haired man with a long beard and small, round glasses standing in what seemed to be a workshop of some kind. In the background was a bench covered in tools and various pieces of metal and wood. The man wore an apron over his clothes, and sitting on one outstretched hand was a doll of some kind. The doll looked like a little old man with brownish skin the color of dried oak leaves. He had a long, crooked nose and a wrinkled face like a withered apple.

He was dressed in red clothes, and had a short, pointed red hat on his head.

"That's a painting of Felix Thatcher," Sasha informed Tucker. "He was an inventor. He lived here a long time ago."

"Did he build the house?" Tucker asked.

Sasha shook his head. "His grandfather did. *His* name was Ahab Thatcher. He owned a bunch of whaling ships a billion years ago. That's why this house is called Stormwatch House. There's a room in one of the towers where you can see all the way to the ocean. Ahab used to go up there to see what the weather was like out at sea. They worried about that kind of thing a lot back then, since there were a lot of shipwrecks."

"So, why is Felix's portrait here and not Ahab's?" asked Tucker.

"It used to be here," Sasha explained. "Then there was a fire. Part of the house burned, including the portrait of Ahab. But Felix was a woodworker, and he rebuilt everything almost exactly like it had been before, so you can't even tell."

"What's that toy he's holding?"

Sasha turned and looked at Tucker. "I don't know if I should tell you," she said. "I know you don't like scary things."

Tucker felt himself blush. Ever since he'd admitted to not reading his mom's books, the other kids sometimes teased him for being afraid. Not in a mean way. More like they were looking out for him. But it still made him feel like he should be braver than he felt.

"It's okay," he said, trying to sound confident. "I mean, how scary can it be?"

"Pretty scary," Sasha warned. "You sure you want to hear it?"

Tucker wasn't sure at all, but he nodded anyway.

"Okay," Sasha said. "Well, like I told you, Felix was a woodworker. He was also a toy-maker. Dolls. Marionettes. Jack-in-the-boxes. All kinds of things."

"How is that scary?" Tucker asked.

"The toys aren't the scary part," said Sasha. "It's how he made them. That thing he's hold-ing? It's a creature called a grelkin. It's a kind of gnome, or troll, or something like that. Supposedly, Felix had a whole bunch of them working for him. They helped build the toys."

"Grelkins?" Tucker said. "I've never heard of anything like that. Where did they come from?"

"One of Ahab's ships," said Sasha. "He

brought them back with him. Or they stowed away on the ship. The story is, the fire that burned this place was started by them because they were angry that Ahab didn't believe in them. See, grelkins are usually invisible. You can only see them with special glasses. Ahab didn't have those, so he never saw the grelkins. That made them mad. Grelkins are like that."

Tucker wasn't sure what to think about Sasha's story. It was pretty ridiculous. It also sounded like some of the stories he'd read about other make-believe creatures, like elves or pixies who helped people make clothes and shoes in exchange for gifts, then pulled pranks when they were ignored or the humans gave them the wrong presents. He suspected Sasha had read the same stories and was making this one up.

"Why did they help Felix, then?" he asked.

Sasha rolled her eyes. "Because," she said as if the answer should be obvious, "he believed in them. He made those glasses he's wearing and—"

"Sasha!" a girl's voice shouted.

Tucker turned his head and saw that a door had opened at the end of the hall. Someone wearing a giant cat head was standing there. "There you are," the girl said. "Come on. You're missing your own party."

"That's totally Ping Zhao," Sasha whispered to Tucker. "But pretend you don't know. And you should probably put your mask on too. We're all supposed to be in disguise."

Tucker wanted to ask her more about Felix Thatcher and how she knew so much about him and the grelkins, but Sasha was already walking toward the open door. As she passed a small table, she picked up a mask that was sitting there—a big black-and-yellow-striped bee's face topped by a tall gold crown—and slipped it over her head. *Of course, she's the birthday girl so she gets to be the queen bee*, Tucker thought as he put his own mask on.

He was dressed in black pants and a black shirt that had scalloped wings sewn on the sleeves. With the mask on, he felt even more batlike. Even though looking through the eyeholes made it a little difficult to see, he was able to maneuver his chair in the direction of the party. Sasha had already gone inside the room, and the sound of people having a good time spilled out into the hall. Tucker couldn't wait to be part of it.

As he neared the door, he thought he saw

something out of the corner of his left eye, a quick movement, as if someone or something had darted past him. He turned his head, but there was no one else in the hallway. He resumed his course for the door, and had almost reached it when something moved on the other side of him. This time, he was sure he saw something, but only for a moment. He wheeled his chair around and looked. But once again, there was nothing there.

He glanced back at the portrait of Felix Thatcher, and his eyes went to the grelkin sitting on the man's hand. It seemed to be looking right at him. Tucker turned away. *It's just a stupid story*, he told himself as he motored quickly toward the ballroom and the party inside.

3

Tucker laughed as Dr. Okafor carefully spun his chair in circles. He was blindfolded, the wide strip of cloth placed over his eyes and tied behind his head making it impossible to know where he was. He could have turned the chair himself, but half the fun of the game was feeling like he was on a carnival ride. The movement made him a little dizzy. It felt great.

"Okay," Dr. Okafor said. "Now try to pin the tail on the donkey."

Tucker moved his chair forward, doing it himself now. He couldn't see where he was going, but he knew he'd been pointed in the general direction of the wall where a paper cut-out of a donkey's body had been taped. In addition to the donkey, there were cutouts of an elephant, a hippo, a bear, and a kangaroo. The goal of the game was for the blindfolded player to place a paper donkey tail on the wall anywhere near the donkey's body, avoiding the other ones. The tail itself rested on Tucker's lap. He was the fourth partygoer to give it a try. Of the other three, only Matty Carpenter had gotten anywhere close to the donkey, and he had pinned the tail on the poor creature's nose.

Tucker kept going until he felt the footrest

of his chair touch something. He reached forward, and his fingertips met a solid surface. He
was at the wall. But was he anywhere close to
the donkey? He couldn't tell. He felt paper,
so he knew he was in front of one of the animals.
But which one? He took the tail and held it
out, pressing it against the wall until it stuck.
Immediately, the other kids started shrieking
with laughter. Tucker reached up and pulled
the blindfold over his head. Then he started
laughing along with his friends. The tail was
stuck in the right place on an animal, but it was
on the bear, not the donkey.

"Tucker invented a bearky!" a girl in a witch
mask shouted, giggling (Tucker could tell by
the red braids sticking out that it was Olivia
Lowrey).

"Good job, Tuck," Sasha said as Tucker

wheeled himself back to the other side of the room. "That's even better than a plain old donkey. I think you win."

"You just want the game to be over so you can open your presents," said a boy whose head was encased in a huge plastic pineapple. Someone wearing a peach head was standing next to him, nodding in agreement, and Tucker guessed they were the twins, George and Andy Shaw, but he wasn't sure which was which.

"What a great idea," Sasha said as if she hadn't been thinking about it at all. "Everybody over to the gift table!"

"I forgot the knife for the cake," her mother said. "I'll be back in a minute."

The kids all went to the other end of the ballroom, where a large table covered with a bee-patterned tablecloth stood covered in gifts.

Beside them, a beehive-shaped cake frosted with yellow icing sat on a cake stand. Looking at it, Tucker hoped Sasha would hurry through the gifts so they could eat.

She didn't. She took her time, opening each thing and exclaiming over it. Every new gift she got was "the greatest ever" and "just what I wanted." She loved the *Animal Crossing* video game from Andy and George. She loved the watercolor paints from Ping. She loved the Badger Johns novel from Olivia. It got to be a joke, so that every time she pulled the paper off a box, everyone shouted, "It's just what I wanted!"

"Well, it *is*," Sasha said, laughing, as she held up Matty's present, a cool journal with a unicorn on the cover.

Sasha scanned the table, looking for any more presents. She frowned. "Where's your present,

Tucker?" she asked. "I thought you put it here when you came in."

"I did," Tucker said. "It was a box wrapped in pink paper with gold polka dots on it."

Sasha lifted up the drifts of discarded paper from the other gifts. She peeked under the table. She searched behind the cake. "That's weird," she said. "It's not here."

The other kids looked at Tucker, as if maybe he'd been wrong about bringing a gift in the first place. Seeing the cat, witch, astronaut, and fruit faces staring at him, he suddenly felt very uncomfortable. "I definitely put it there," he said firmly.

"Who's ready for cake?" Sasha's mother asked, sweeping into the room.

Everyone else seemed to forget about the missing present as they took their masks off

(Tucker saw now that the peach was George and the pineapple was Andy) and crowded around the cake. Dr. Okafor opened a box of candles and started placing them all over the beehive. When there were eleven of them on the cake, she looked around the table. "That's strange," she said. "I thought I set a box of matches here to light the candles with."

They all helped her look, but there were no matches to be found. Watching everyone search, Tucker started to get a weird feeling. His present going missing was strange enough. Now something else was gone. Who—or what—had taken them? His thoughts flashed back to the odd moment in the hallway earlier. Maybe he *had* seen something after all.

Just then, Sasha's dad came walking into the room. He shook something in his hand. "You left this box of matches in the kitchen," he told his wife. "I thought you might need them."

With the missing matches found, Dr. Okafor lit the candles on the cake. Sasha stood in front of it. "Make a wish," her father said.

Sasha closed her eyes. A moment later, she leaned in and blew hard. The candles went out one by one, until all of them had been extinguished and the air was filled with little tendrils of smoke.

"What did you wish for?" Olivia asked her.

"If I tell you, it won't come true," said Sasha as her dad began cutting the cake and putting the slices on plates. "But it *might* have been for a kitten."

The cake was delicious, and by the time he finished his slice, the weird feeling in Tucker's belly had been replaced by a sense of sugary happiness. He even forgot about the missing present and what he might or might not have seen in the hallway, especially when Sasha said, "Who wants to see Felix's workshop?"

Everybody did. They all filed out into yet another hallway (the ballroom had half a dozen doors) and Sasha led them to what looked like an ordinary piece of wall paneling. But then she touched a spot on it and it swung open, revealing a set of stairs. "The workshop is down there," she said. As the others started to go down, she turned to Tucker, who was looking at the steep stairs and wondering how he would get down them. "Don't worry," Sasha said. "There's an elevator that you can use. Only it's kind of small."

"How small?" Tucker asked.

"It will probably only fit you, so you'll have

to go alone," said Sasha. "I'll meet you at the bottom, okay?"

Tucker hesitated. The thought of being alone in a small space wasn't very appealing. And what if the elevator got stuck? He felt the uneasy feeling coming back. He pushed it down. He wanted to see the workshop. He nodded.

Sasha opened a second door beside the first one. This one was smaller than the other, and behind it was a space just big enough for Tucker to roll his chair into. He turned the chair around and rolled back. Sure enough, he was able to get the chair inside with only enough room left for the door to close again.

"The buttons are over there," Sasha said, pointing. "I'll see you in a minute. And don't worry about the flickering lights. It's a short ride."

Before Tucker could ask her what she meant

about the lights, she shut the door. Then he understood. It was dim inside the tiny elevator, and the lights pulsated a little. He almost called out for Sasha to let him out. Instead, he pushed hard on the button. He heard the machine whir to life, and a moment later it started to descend.

Then it stopped. The lights flickered again, before sputtering completely out. At first, he thought he was at the bottom already, and waited for Sasha to open the door. When nothing happened, he called out. "Sasha? Are you there?"

The only answer was what sounded like laughter. Then Tucker heard something moving around in the elevator. Something small. It made scratching sounds as it scuttled around somewhere underneath his chair.

"Hello?" Tucker said.

There was no answer.

"Sasha!" he shouted. "Somebody!"

Then he was sure he heard an old, rusty voice whisper, "Can you see me now?"

He jerked the lever up and down, up and down, frantically trying to get the elevator to move. The elevator dropped. Tucker breathed in and out rapidly, trying not to panic and not doing a very good job of it. Then the door in front of him finally slid open and Sasha and his other friends were standing there.

"Get it away from me!" Tucker yelped, moving his chair out into the light so quickly that everyone scattered to get out of his way.

"Get what away from you?" Sasha asked. "There's nothing there, Tuck. See?"

Tucker looked down. The elevator was empty. The others stared at him, just as they had when they heard that his present was missing.

"I think there's a rat in there," he muttered, looking at the shadowy interior of the elevator and hoping a whiskered rodent would scurry out and make him feel better. None did.

"Well, you're okay now," Sasha said, obviously trying to cheer him up. "Welcome to the workshop!"

Tucker tore his gaze away from the elevator. But even as he took in the marvelous sight of the room around him, he heard a voice like a chill breeze whisper in his ear, "Can you see me now?"

4

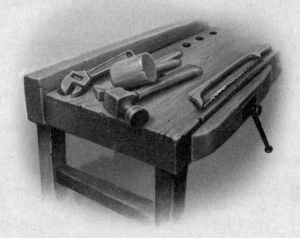

Felix Thatcher's workshop looked just like it did in the painting in the upstairs hallway. The room was large, and there were several wooden benches placed around it, all of them covered with tools, sawdust, and scraps of wood and metal. Partially completed projects sat here and there, like carved wooden figures that were missing their heads or limbs, windup toys with gears and springs piled beside them, and other interesting-looking things that mystified Tucker. Pages of notes written in messy, impossible-to-read handwriting and covered in rough sketches were scattered here and there alongside rags that were splattered with splotches of paint. It looked as if Felix had recently been working there, not like he'd been dead for more than a hundred years.

"How come nobody has cleaned up in here?" Ping asked, running a finger over one of the workbench tops.

"It's much more interesting like this," Sasha answered. "Besides, the grelkins wouldn't like it."

At the mention of the creatures, Tucker felt himself stiffen. He'd just started to shake off what had happened in the elevator. Now it all came back to him—the feeling that something had been in the elevator with him, the whispery voice.

"Come on," said Andy. "You don't really believe those stories, do you?"

"Sure I do," Sasha said. "All *kinds* of weird things happen in this house."

Tucker guessed that Sasha had shown each of them the painting when they arrived, and told them all the same story. He didn't feel like hearing her talk about the stupid grelkins anymore, so while she and Andy started to argue about whether or not the things were real, he wheeled himself away from them, distracting himself by examining some of the objects that were on the workbenches.

He was rolling along when he heard something crinkle. Looking down, he saw that he had wheeled over a crumpled-up piece of paper. Something about it was familiar. He leaned over and saw that it was the wrapping paper from the gift he'd brought for Sasha. It had been torn off the box, along with the bow he'd placed on top, which was lying a few feet away. But how had they gotten down here?

The sound of giggling startled him. He glanced around, thinking one of his friends must be laughing at something, but they were all busy talking in other parts of the workshop. The giggling had definitely sounded close by. He looked around, but there was nobody there. At least nobody that he could see.

As he was trying to peer behind a bench, he heard a shout. He looked up and saw Sasha pulling something out of her hair. She looked angry. "What is this?" she said.

More giggling filled the air as Tucker wheeled his chair closer to the others. Then he saw what Sasha was holding. "It's a dart," he said.

Sasha peered at the thing in her hand. "A dart?"

"See, there's Velcro on the tip," Tucker said. "There's a dartboard that hangs on the wall. You throw the darts at it and they stick."

"Where did it come from?" Sasha asked.

"Um, I think it's my present," said Tucker. "The one that went missing. I found the wrapping paper over there." He pointed to the wad of paper still lying on the floor behind him.

Sasha frowned. "Well, how did it get down—hey!" She squawked as another dart sailed through the air and landed in her hair.

"I did it," a weird voice announced.

They all turned in the direction of the sound. At one of the benches, a small figure just like the one in the painting stood, staring at them. "You don't belong here," it said in a raspy voice.

"This workshop belongs to Felix Thatcher. Get out!"

Ice-cold fear flooded through Tucker. The voice sounded exactly like the one in the elevator. "It's a grelkin!" he yelped. "They're real!"

The grelkin giggled. It danced from side to side.

"We have to get out of here!" Tucker shouted. "Come on!"

The grelkin giggled again and hopped up and down. Tucker started to wheel himself back toward the elevator, but Sasha stormed over to the creature and, to Tucker's horror, snatched it off the workbench.

"Hey!" the grelkin shouted.

Sasha looked under the workbench. "It's no grelkin," she said. "Eke, get out from under there."

A little boy scrambled out from under the table. Sasha took him by the arm and led him back to the group. "Everybody, this is my little brother, Eke. He was *supposed* to be up in his room, watching a movie."

"I got bored," Eke said, pulling his arm away from his sister. Then he looked at Tucker and grinned widely. "I got you good," he said. He imitated Tucker, yelling, "It's a grelkin! They're real!" He laughed. Some of the other kids laughed too.

"I was just playing along," Tucker said. "I knew it wasn't real."

"Sure," Eke said. He looked at Sasha. "Is there any cake left?"

Sasha sighed. "Go ask Mom," she said, and Eke ran off. Sasha set the toy grelkin down on the bench, where it fell over sideways and lay there, its painted eyes staring at Tucker. Tucker looked away as Sasha came over and put her hand on his shoulder. "He's always doing stuff like that," she said. "Don't worry about it."

Tucker nodded, but he didn't feel any better. He felt stupid for being so scared. He snuck a glance at the toy grelkin. *It's just a doll*, he told himself. *It's made out of wood. And Sasha made up the whole story about them. There's no such thing as grelkins.*

Now that Eke had ruined the mood, Tucker waited impatiently for the others to be finished looking around the workshop. He was relieved when they finally decided to go back upstairs. At least until he remembered that he would have to go into the elevator again. To his relief, though, nothing weird happened this time, and soon he was back in the ballroom.

Eke came over to him, holding a plate with a piece of cake on it. "Sorry I scared you," he said, chewing. "It was just a joke."

"It's okay," Tucker told him. "You make a great grelkin."

Eke laughed. "You should have seen your face," he said.

"You shouldn't have taken my present," Sasha said sternly.

Her brother shook his head. "I didn't," he said.

Sasha put her hands on her hips. "How did it get down there, then?" she asked.

Eke shrugged and took another bite of cake. "I don't know," he said. "It was there when I got there. I found it on the workbench. The bow was off, and one corner was ripped. It looked like someone had been trying to open it." He gasped. "Maybe it was a grelkin!" he said, then laughed and walked off.

"He's going to be in so much trouble," Sasha said to Tucker. "Of course he took it."

"Right," Tucker agreed. "I mean, how else could it have gotten down there?"

For the next hour, they played more party games and had a good time. Tucker joined in, but he didn't have as much fun as everybody else seemed to be having. He kept thinking about the grelkin on the workbench, about the voice in the elevator, and about the missing present. He wanted to believe that Eke had taken it. But he said he hadn't.

When Sasha's dad came over and told him that his mother had arrived to take him home, Tucker was ready to leave. He said goodbye to everyone, then wheeled himself down the hall toward the front doors. As he passed the portrait of Felix Thatcher, he avoided looking at it.

In the entryway, he found his mother talking to Dr. Okafor.

"Hey," his mom said. "How was the party?"

"Great!" Tucker said, trying to sound enthusiastic. "We had a lot of fun."

"Dr. Okafor and I were just discussing the history of the house," his mother said. "It's so fascinating."

"I'd be happy to give you a tour," Sasha's mother said.

"I would love that!" said Tucker's mom.

"My stomach is feeling a little weird," Tucker said quickly. He put his hand on his belly and made a face. "I probably shouldn't have had that third piece of cake."

His mother looked worried. "We should get you home," she said.

"Another time, then," Dr. Okafor said. "And remind your husband to call me about the plumbing."

Tucker and his mother were almost out the door when Sasha came running up, holding out the bat mask. "You forgot this," she said.

"Thanks," Tucker said, taking it from her. "I'll see you at school on Monday."

Outside, it was already getting dark. Once he was settled in the van, Tucker felt better. As his mother started up the engine, he picked up the bat mask and held it to his face. He looked at the house, peering through the eyes in the bat's wings. The front door was shut. Then it opened, just a crack. He thought Sasha might appear, or one of the other kids. Instead, a small

shadow slipped out. The door shut again. Whatever had come out moved quickly in the direction
of the van. But in the gloom, Tucker couldn't tell
what it was.

It's just a cat, he told himself as his mother
started to drive away. *It's just a cat*.

But he wished she would drive faster.

5

Great-Aunt Hilda smelled like baby powder, roses, and eucalyptus cough drops. As she hugged Tucker tightly, kissing him on both cheeks, he held his breath as she said something in Swedish that sounded like a question.

"Sorry," Tucker said when she released him. "All I know how to say is '*Var är toaletten?*'"

"'Where is the toilet?'" Great-Aunt Hilda translated. "That is a very important thing to know how to say. Maybe I can teach you a few more things while I'm here."

"What smells so good?" Tucker's mother asked, sniffing.

"Swedish meatballs," Great-Aunt Hilda said. "Or as we call them in Sweden, meatballs. They're almost ready."

Tucker went to his room, where he placed the bat mask on his bedside table. Then he wheeled his chair into the adjoining bathroom and washed his hands at the sink. It had been an eventful day, and he wasn't sure what to think about everything that had happened. Parts of it had been great, and other parts had been not so great. Overall, though, he'd had fun with his friends, and that was what he decided to focus on.

At dinner, Great-Aunt Hilda asked him a million questions about school, his friends, and other things in his life. "I hear you are going to be the star of the school musical," she said.

"I'm *probably* going to be in the musical," Tucker said. "I'm hoping I get to be the Cowardly Lion."

Great-Aunt Hilda nodded. "He was always my favorite," she said. "Everybody could use a little extra courage, I think. Sing me a little bit of your audition song."

Tucker cleared his throat and sang her a few lines from "If I Were King of the Forest." When he was done, everyone clapped. "Wonderful," Great-Aunt Hilda proclaimed. "I will come back when it's time for the play."

After dinner, Tucker's father helped Great-Aunt Hilda clean up while Tucker's mom helped him get ready for bed. When he was tucked in, his cat, Gustopher, padded into the room and jumped up on the bed, curling into a ball beside him.

"He's had a hard day not catching any mice," Tucker's mother joked. She kissed Tucker on the forehead. "Don't stay up too late reading," she said.

Tucker promised not to. His mother left, and he picked up the graphic novel he was reading and opened it. As he turned the pages, he rubbed Gustopher's ears. The cat responded by purring loudly.

"I bet if there were any grelkins in our house, you'd take care of them," Tucker said as Gustopher stretched out one striped paw and twitched his tail.

"Grelkins?" said a voice from the doorway. Great-Aunt Hilda came into the room. "What is a grelkin?"

"Oh, um, just something I heard about," Tucker said.

Great-Aunt Hilda sat down on the edge of the bed. Gustopher lazily opened one gold eye, looked at her for a moment, then shut it again. "Tell me about them," she said.

"Okay," Tucker said. "Well, I *think* they're like elves. They're small, and sometimes they help people make stuff."

"Ah," Great-Aunt Hilda said. "They sound a bit like tomtar."

"Tomtar?" said Tucker.

"Little men who help around the house and help farmers care for livestock," Great-Aunt Hilda explained.

"So, tomtar are good?" said Tucker. He hoped that if grelkins were related to them, they might be the same.

"Mostly," Great-Aunt Hilda said. "Like all of the little people, they are unpredictable. They can have very bad tempers if they feel you have wronged them."

"Have you ever heard of tomtar coming to this country?" Tucker asked, thinking about what Sasha had said about grelkins. "Like, on a ship, maybe?"

"I don't see why they couldn't," Great-Aunt Hilda said. "If my parents could, anybody could. My mother was seasick the entire journey, but she made it." She laughed. "What makes you ask about these grelkins?"

Tucker considered telling her the whole story. But he was getting tired. Also, he was kind of afraid that if he started talking about everything that had happened at Stormwatch House, he might get nervous all over again. "I just read about them somewhere," he said.

Great-Aunt Hilda nodded. "Well," she said. "If grelkins are like tomtar, they will not stay long in the house if there is a cat. They are terrible enemies."

"Really?" Tucker said. "They'd be afraid of Gustopher?"

"Very afraid," Great-Aunt Hilda assured him. "You have nothing to worry about."

Even though he was still mostly sure that grelkins were make-believe, Tucker felt better.

"Anyway, I came to say good night," Great-Aunt Hilda said. "And now I will. You have a good sleep. Tomorrow I will show you how to bake *vaniljkakor*. Swedish jam cookies."

"Great!" Tucker said as he was once again engulfed in Great-Aunt Hilda's powdery scent.

When his great-aunt was gone, he decided

he was too tired to keep reading. He turned off the light and closed his eyes. Resting his hand on Gustopher's back, he yawned. "You're on guard duty," he told the cat.

He dreamed about wandering through the halls of Stormwatch House. The electricity was out, and he didn't have a flashlight, so the only illumination was the lightning that flashed outside the windows. He was rolling his chair down the long hallway, trying to find someone to help him, when he heard a voice. "Can you see me now?" it asked.

Tucker woke up. Frantically, he felt around the bed for his cat. "Gustopher?" he whispered. "Gustopher, where are you?"

Something moved on the floor. "Can you see me now?" the voice from his dream said.

Only he wasn't dreaming now. He was awake.

Tucker reached for the light on his bedside table. In his panic, he knocked it with his hand. The lamp fell to the floor, and he heard the bulb shatter. Now the only light in his room came from the window. But the moon was just a tiny sliver in the sky, and it filled his room with shadows.

"Gustopher!" Tucker hissed, still moving his hand around the bedside table, as if there might be something there that would help him. His fingers touched something. It was the bat mask. Instinctively, he picked it up and pressed it against his face.

"Can you see me now?" The voice sounded closer.

Tucker looked around. And now he *could* see something. On the rug below, barely visible in the thin moonlight, was a small figure. A small figure wearing a pointed hat. Tucker gasped. The figure moved toward him, one step at a time. It reached out a tiny hand. Tucker felt his heart beat faster. He pulled the mask away from his face.

The figure disappeared.

Tucker put the mask on again, and once more he could see the shadowy form moving steadily across the floor. It got close enough that he could see its face. The tiny, dark eyes stared at him without blinking. "You can see me now," the voice creaked. Tucker thought the withered mouth turned up in a faint smile. He tried to drop the mask so that he wouldn't have to look at the horrible thing, but he was frozen with fear.

"Meow!"

Gustopher leaped into the room. He arched

his back and hissed. One paw swept out, hitting the grelkin, which staggered backward but didn't fall over. Gustopher swiped at it again, missing. The grelkin ran quickly to the doorway. Tucker heard the sound of footsteps as it retreated down the hall.

Gustopher came over to him and sat down, staring at the empty doorway. Tucker half hoped the cat would chase after the grelkin, but he also didn't want to be left alone in the dark. He stroked Gustopher's head. "Good boy," he said, finally finding his voice.

He didn't know what to do. He could call for his parents. But what would he tell them? That a fairy-tale monster was running around their house? They would never believe that. They would say he'd had a bad dream because of the story Sasha had told him.

Then he thought about the mask. He'd been able to see the grelkin only when he put it on. Sasha had said that only people with magic glasses could see grelkins. And the man at the store had said something about bats being able to see things other animals couldn't. Was the mask acting like a pair of magic glasses?

He put the mask in front of his face again and looked around the room. Nothing seemed different. But he had definitely seen the grelkin when he was wearing it. He slipped the mask's string over his head, securing it in place. Then he leaned back against the pillows. He continued to pet Gustopher as he lay there in the dark, waiting for morning to come.

6

"I think maybe that is too much jam for one cookie."

Tucker looked down at the tray of *vaniljka-kor* sitting on the table in front of him. Each cookie was dusted with powdered sugar and had an indentation in the center. He was supposed to be filling these hollows with spoonfuls of raspberry jam. But he wasn't paying attention, and had overfilled one of them so that sticky fruit was dripping over the side and onto the cookie sheet.

"Sorry," he said.

Great-Aunt Hilda picked the cookie up and popped it into her mouth. "It tastes just as delicious as the perfect ones," she said kindly.

Tucker went back to work. He was having a good time, but he was also tired from being up most of the night. He really wished he could lie down and take a nap. But he was afraid to close his eyes, in case the grelkin from the night before was still around. He thought Gustopher might have scared it away, as there hadn't been any sign of it in the house. Still, he was anxious. Now that he knew grelkins were real, and that one had apparently followed him home from Sasha's party, he had no idea what to do about it.

He'd kept the bat mask nearby all day. It

was in the hanging bag on the side of his wheel-chair, where he usually stored things like his schoolbooks and supplies. Every so often, he put the mask on and looked around whatever room he was in. Each time, his heart sped up a little as he anticipated seeing the grelkin standing on a table or sitting on top of the television. So far, though, he'd seen nothing out of the ordinary.

He finished filling the *vaniljkakor*, screwed the top back on the jar of jam, and stuck it in the refrigerator. As he shut the fridge door, his mother came into the kitchen. "Your father and I are taking Great-Aunt Hilda to the local history museum to see a quilt display," she said. "Do you want to come?"

Tucker really wasn't interested in seeing a bunch of quilts. He also wasn't very thrilled about the idea of being home alone. *Then again,* he thought, *it might give him some time to search for the grelkin some more without his parents wondering what he was up to.* "No," he said. "I have some math homework to do before school tomorrow. I'll stay here."

"Okay," his mother said as she picked up her purse and keys from the kitchen counter. "Have fun. We'll bring back dinner from Dragon-Dragon. Do you want chicken with string beans?"

"And hot and sour soup, please," Tucker said.

When the adults were gone, he took the bat mask and put it on. He coaxed Gustopher onto his lap by rattling a container of tuna-flavored Kitty Nibbles, then proceeded to patrol the house room by room. There was no sign of the grelkin anywhere. Relieved, Tucker removed the mask and wheeled himself back into the living room.

Gustopher jumped down, then ran to the door and started to butt the cat flap that led to the outside with his head. He stopped, sniffed, then hissed. His fur stuck up all over his body, and he backed away from the flap. His ears were flat against his head, and his tail twitched angrily.

"What is it?" Tucker asked.

He wheeled over and looked at the cat flap. A scrap of red fabric was stuck in it. Tucker took out the grabbing stick he kept in his chair's side pocket and used it to pinch the cloth between its metal fingers. He tugged, and it came free from the cat flap. As soon as it was gone, Gustopher dashed through the flap and out into the yard.

Tucker dropped the thing into his hand and looked at it. It was a hat. A short, pointed hat exactly like the one the grelkin was wearing in the portrait of Felix Thatcher, and that he'd seen on the head of the grelkin in his bedroom the night before. Just touching it sent shivers down his back.

"Give me my cap."

The voice came from behind him. Tucker turned the chair around. He didn't see anything. Then he held the bat mask up to his face. The grelkin was standing on the table in the kitchen, which was open to the living room. Its head was bare.

"You stole my cap," the grelkin said.

"I didn't steal it," said Tucker, his voice shaking. "It looks like you got it caught in the cat door when you were coming in or going out."

"Thief!" the grelkin shouted.

"I'm not a thief!" Tucker shouted back.

"Rogue!" the grelkin growled. It put its hands on its hips and glared hard at him. "Cutpurse!"

"I don't even know what that word means," Tucker said.

"You stole my cap," the grelkin said. "I will have my revenge." It bent down and picked up one of the *vaniljkakor*. Cocking its arm, it hurled it at Tucker, who ducked. The cookie hit the wall behind him, crumbling and leaving a smear of raspberry jam behind.

"Hey!" Tucker cried. "Knock it off, or you'll never get your hat back."

This announcement seemed to make the grelkin even angrier. It picked up another *vaniljkaka* and threw it at Tucker, then another. A volley of cookies came at him, each one sending raspberry jam and powdered sugar everywhere. It was on the wall, on the floor, and on Tucker.

"Rapscallion!" the little grelkin bellowed. "Scoundrel!"

Tucker didn't know what to do. The grelkin kept pelting him with cookies. He had to get away. He dropped the bat mask onto his lap, put his hands on the rims of his wheels, and pushed. He turned his head. The grelkin had disappeared, and now it looked like some invisible force was lifting the *vaniljkakor* from the cookie sheet and sending them sailing through the air.

Tucker rolled down the hallway. Behind him, he heard the sound of the grelkin running. Its tiny feet smacked against the wood as it chased after him. He pushed harder, and the chair flew through the door of his bedroom. Tucker grabbed the edge of the door as he passed by and shoved it. The door slammed shut with a bang. A second later, the sound of small fists hitting it echoed through the room.

"Give me my cap, thief!" the grelkin yelled.

Tucker turned his chair around and sat there, staring at the door from a safe distance. The grelkin wasn't tall enough to reach the handle to open it, but Tucker used the grabbing stick to lock it anyway. The creature continued to pound on the door. It also sounded like he was now kicking it.

Tucker was holding the hat in his hand. He realized he was worrying it between his fingers, pulling anxiously at the material. Then he felt it rip. A long tear appeared, running halfway up the side of the hat. Tucker threw it on the floor.

Then he used his stick to push it partway through the narrow crack under the door.

"There's your stupid hat!" he called out. "Now leave me alone!"

He saw the hat get pulled the rest of the way out into the hall. Then the grelkin howled furiously. "Ruined!" it screamed. "Spoiled!"

"I didn't mean to," Tucker shouted. "It was an accident."

"Deceiver!" the grelkin said, kicking the door so hard that it rattled. "Liar!"

"I'm going to call the cat!" Tucker said. "Gustopher!"

The noise stopped. Tucker waited for it to start up again, but it didn't.

"Hello?" he called out.

There was no response. Still, he waited a long time before going to the door and unlocking it.

He pulled it open a crack and looked into the hall. It was empty. The grelkin was gone. Tucker breathed a sigh of relief. Apparently, the creature had decided that getting its hat back was enough. "A hat I didn't steal in the first place," Tucker muttered as he rolled into the hallway.

He figured he had enough time to clean up the mess in the other room before his parents got home. However, before he could pick up even one cookie or clean one spot of jam off the wall, the front door opened and his mother walked in.

"The quilt display ended yesterday, apparently, and we didn't really want to look at a bunch of butter churns, so—" His mother stopped speaking and looked around the room. The bag of food from Dragon-Dragon swung from her hand, the smell of chicken with string beans and moo shu pork filling the air. "What happened?" she asked. Behind her, Tucker's dad and Great-Aunt Hilda peered over her shoulder, their eyes wide.

"Um," Tucker said. "Would you believe a freak windstorm blew through and sent the *vaniljkakor* flying?"

"No," his mother said. "I would not."

"Squirrels?" Tucker suggested. "Ghosts?"

"No and no," said his mother. "Now, what really happened?"

Tucker sighed. He didn't need a fortune cookie from Dragon-Dragon to tell him that his luck had taken a turn for the worse.

7

When Tucker arrived at school on Monday morning, he was in a rotten mood. Because he'd been afraid that his parents would think he was making up the story about the grelkin, he had instead blamed the incident with the *vaniljka-kor* on poor Gustopher, telling them that the cat had jumped up on the table and scattered the cookies everywhere. Nobody had been mad about it, but Tucker felt bad for not telling the truth. But there was no way he was going to tell anyone that a supposedly make-believe little man had done it. Besides, now that the grelkin had his hat, he was most likely gone for good.

As he approached his classroom, Tucker noticed a group of kids standing in front of the door to the drama teacher's room. At first, he was confused. Then he remembered that the cast list for *The Wizard of Oz* was supposed to be posted that day. He had forgotten all about it. Seeing the paper taped to the door, he started to get excited, wondering if his name would be on it.

"Ping is Dorothy!" Sasha announced. She was right at the front of the pack, running her finger down the list. "And I'm Glinda."

"What are we?" Andy and George asked in unison.

Sasha laughed. "What else," she said, "flying monkeys!"

Tucker was afraid to ask if his name was up there with the others. He almost didn't want to look. But then Sasha saw him. "I hope you've been practicing your roar, Tuck, because you're the Cowardly Lion."

Tucker pumped his fist and gave his best impression of a lion. George and Andy both gave him high fives, then went back to pretending to be monkeys. Tucker was so happy that he forgot all about his bad mood as he wheeled the rest of the way to his classroom and over to his desk.

"I know you're all super excited about the musical," Mr. Batson said as the other kids filed in, chatting loudly. "And congratulations to all of you. You're going to have your first cast meeting with Ms. Chartier in a little bit. Before that, though, we're going to work on our science projects."

Although Tucker couldn't wait to start rehearsals for the musical, he was also excited about his science project. For the past month, he had been working on building a model of a volcano. He retrieved the model from the back of the classroom and brought it to his desk. In the crater of the volcano he had placed an empty plastic bottle. When it was time to make the volcano erupt, he would add baking soda, laundry detergent, and red food coloring to the bottle. Then he would pour in vinegar. The chemical reaction would make a bubbly, lavalike substance that would rise up and flow over the sides of the volcano. Tucker was excited about seeing if it would really work. For now, the ingredients were stored in little containers so that they wouldn't accidentally mix.

As he put the finishing touches on the volcano's paint job, Tucker thought about how much fun it was going to be starring in the school musical. He imagined opening night, with his parents and maybe Great-Aunt Hilda sitting in the audience, watching him sing and dance as he traveled down the yellow brick road with Dorothy, the Tin Man, and the Scarecrow on the way to the Emerald City. He was particularly looking forward to his big solo, and he hummed the music to it while he painted.

Olivia, whose desk was next to his and who had gotten the role of the Tin Man, started humming along with him. Her science project was about seeds. In addition to actually sprouting several different kinds, she had drawn detailed pictures of the insides of each one. Tucker looked over at them.

"Wow," he said. "Those are fantastic."

"Thanks," said Olivia. "I love to draw and paint. I'm hoping Ms. Chartier will let me help with the sets for the show."

When the bell rang a few minutes later, everybody left their science projects on their desks and went down the hall to Ms. Chartier's room. She handed out packets containing the script and music for *The Wizard of Oz*, and for the next forty-five minutes they read over their lines and went over the rehearsal schedule.

"This is going to be so awesome," Ping said as they walked back to Mr. Batson's room.

Her expression changed as soon as she saw the inside of the room. There was foamy red liquid covering the desktops. It streaked the walls and ran in sticky streams between the desks. Olivia tiptoed through the mess to her desk and snatched up one of her drawings, which was smeared with the stuff. "It's ruined!" she wailed. "They're *all* ruined!"

Mr. Batson entered the room behind them. "What happened in here?" he asked. "I went to the teachers' lounge to get a cup of coffee, and everything was fine when I left."

"It's Tucker's volcano," Olivia said. She pointed to his desk, where the volcano was indeed covered in the foamy fake lava. Some of it was still bubbling out of the crater.

"I didn't do it," Tucker said as everybody turned to stare at him. "I had everything in separate containers. They weren't even open."

"Are you sure you maybe didn't leave them where they might have accidentally fallen over and gotten mixed together?" Mr. Batson asked. "I'm not saying you did it on purpose. But maybe—"

"No!" Tucker shouted. He was upset now, and felt himself shaking. He hated being accused of something that he hadn't done.

"Okay," said Mr. Batson, putting his hand on Tucker's shoulder. "Well, we're going to need to get this room cleaned up. I'll go get the janitor. In the meantime, everybody head over to the art room. It's not being used right now."

Tucker tried not to look at Olivia, who was holding her dripping drawings in her hands and seemed like she might start crying at any second. He tried not to look at anybody. Even if their science projects weren't spoiled by the volcano's eruption, their desks and chairs were still a mess. And even though Tucker was pretty sure Mr. Batson believed him, he worried that not all of his classmates did.

He held back, waiting until everyone else

was out of the classroom and he was alone. He looked over at his desk. The containers of baking soda, vinegar, and food dye were toppled over, their lids scattered and their contents pooled on the desk. Then he noticed something really odd. On the surface of the desk, there was what looked like a line of tiny red footprints. They might have just been blobs of food coloring, but they seemed too evenly spaced.

Tucker followed the prints. They ended at the edge of his desk, started again on Olivia's, then showed up on her chair and on the floor beneath it. Then they made a line for the door, getting fainter and fainter until they disappeared altogether, possibly as the food coloring wore off. Looking at them, Tucker felt his stomach begin to churn.

He opened the bag on the side of his

wheelchair and reached inside. Taking out the mask, which he'd stowed there the night before, he tentatively held it to his face and looked around the room. Standing on Mr. Batson's desk was the grelkin.

"Thief!" the little man said.

"I gave you your hat back!" Tucker said. "You're even wearing it. Why don't you leave me alone?"

The grelkin did indeed have a red hat on. And it looked good as new. Tucker didn't understand why it was still angry at him.

"Scoundrel!" said a voice. Only this one was coming from a different direction.

Tucker turned his head. Standing on his desk was another grelkin. Although it looked exactly like the first one, this one did not have a hat on its head. It held up the container of baking soda and shook it tauntingly.

There are two of them now, Tucker thought miserably.

"Scallywag!" said a third voice.

Tucker looked. Another grelkin was standing on top of Sasha's desk. It was holding one of the glass jars filled with salt crystals that Sasha had grown for her science experiment. It dropped the jar, which fell to the floor and shattered.

"Stop it!" Tucker shouted. "Get out of here!"

The grelkins laughed. It sounded like the wind rustling through leaves on a cold night. Tucker hated it.

"Go on!" he shouted again. "Go!"

"What's all the yelling?" a voice asked. "And why do you have that mask on your face? Are you all right?"

Mr. Bykov, the janitor, was rolling a bucket and

mop into the room. He stopped beside Tucker's wheelchair and whistled. "What a mess," he said. "You did this all yourself, did you?"

"I didn't do it at all," Tucker said. He pointed at the grelkins one at a time. "They did."

But of course Mr. Bykov couldn't see them any more than anyone else could. He nodded and raised one thick black eyebrow. "Okay, okay," he said, rubbing his chin. "Well, I need to get this cleaned up, so you go along with the rest, all right?"

Tucker thought he should warn the man about the grelkins, which were all still there, staring right at him with menacing scowls on their faces. But what was the point? He was going to have to figure out another way to deal with the tiny monsters.

He just had no idea what that was.

8

Great-Aunt Hilda had made another batch of *vaniljkakor*, but even eating six of them didn't make Tucker feel any better.

"Bad day at school?" Great-Aunt Hilda asked as Tucker picked up a seventh cookie and ate it in two bites.

"The worst day," Tucker said. "Everybody is mad at me for something that wasn't my fault."

"I'm sure they will forget all about it soon enough," Great-Aunt Hilda said.

"I don't think so," Tucker told her. "This was pretty bad."

"But your mother says you got a part in the musical," Great-Aunt Hilda said. "That's very exciting."

Tucker shrugged. "I guess."

It *was* exciting, but right then he didn't feel very excited. He felt angry and sad. All day, even after their room was cleaned up and they could go back, the other kids had acted as if he wasn't telling the truth about the volcano. A lot of them were going to have to start their projects all over again, and Tucker felt responsible for that even though it was the grelkins who had caused the explosion.

As for the grelkins, they had disappeared. At

least, Tucker assumed they had. It would have been weird if he'd kept putting the mask on to look for them. But nothing else weird had happened. Not yet, anyway. What Tucker was really afraid of was that the creatures were planning something even worse than what they'd done that morning.

His father came into the kitchen, carrying his bag of plumbing tools. "I just got a call from Mr. Okafor," he said. "One of their pipes has sprung a leak, and I need to go over there and fix it. Want to come along?"

Tucker started to say no. He was afraid Sasha was still mad at him, since her project was one of the ones the grelkins had totally destroyed. Then an idea came to him. "Okay," he said.

"Great," his father said. "Let's go."

When they arrived at Stormwatch House,

Sasha's father met them at the door. "Thank goodness you're here," he said. "There have been two more leaks since I called you. I don't know what's going on in this house, but we need to fix it before it turns into an aquarium."

Tucker's dad went off with Mr. Okafor, leaving Tucker alone in the hallway. Tucker rolled his chair down to where the portrait of Felix Thatcher hung on the wall. He sat there, looking up at it. The grelkin in Felix's hand seemed to look back at him. Tucker stuck out his tongue at it. "I'll figure out a way to stop you," he said to it.

"Are you talking to a painting?"

Tucker turned his head to see who was speaking to him. Sasha was standing a little way off.

"Uh . . . no?" he said.

"Yes, you were," Sasha said. "What did you

mean about finding a way to stop him? The guy's been dead for practically forever."

"Not him," Tucker said. He hesitated, trying to decide how much to tell Sasha. He took a deep breath. "The grelkin."

"The grelkin?" said Sasha. "Grelkins aren't real. They're just a story someone made up to scare little kids."

Tucker shook his head. "They're real," he told her. "They stole my present. One followed me home. And they're the ones who caused the accident at school today."

Sasha sighed. "Come on, Tuck," she said. "I know you're upset about that. And yeah, some people are mad about it. But nobody thinks you did it on purpose, okay? We know you wouldn't do that."

"Thanks," said Tucker. "That actually does

make me feel better. But grelkins are still real. It's like you said—they're invisible unless you have magic glasses. Or this." He took the bat mask out of his carrier and held it up.

"Your mask from the party?" Sasha said.

"I'm telling you, it's magic," he said. "It lets you see things you can't normally see."

Sasha looked doubtful, but she didn't say anything. Tucker knew she was intrigued by his story, even if she wouldn't admit it.

"I can prove it," Tucker assured her.

"How?"

"Let's go down to the workshop," Tucker suggested. "I bet that's where they live most of the time. If you put the mask on, you'll be able to see them."

Sasha bit her lip. "Okay," she said.

She walked beside Tucker as they went

toward the ballroom, then through there into the hallway where the door to the workshop stairs was. "*If* grelkins are real, why did they do that to the classroom today?" Sasha asked as she opened the door to the little elevator.

"They think I stole one of their hats and ripped it," Tucker said.

"Did you?"

"No," Tucker answered. "I mean, I ripped it, but it was an accident. They don't believe me, though. It's stupid."

"No," said Sasha. "I totally get it. One time, Ping borrowed my brand-new ski hat that I got on our family trip to Colorado and she spilled nail polish all over it and ruined it. I knew it was an accident, but I didn't talk to her for like a week. People can get weird about stuff like that. I guess grelkins can too."

Tucker wasn't sure that not talking to some-one was *quite* the same as having a bunch of invisible mini-men coming after you and doing things to get you in trouble, but he didn't say so. Sasha was willing to go along with his plan to look for the grelkins, and that was the most important thing. He took a deep breath to steady his nerves, then backed his chair into the small elevator.

This time, no voices teased him on the way down, and the elevator rode smoothly to the bottom. Sasha opened the door, and Tucker rolled into the workroom. It looked just as it had the day of her birthday.

"What now?" Sasha asked.

Tucker handed her the mask. "Put it on and look around," he instructed. "If there are grel-kins here, you'll be able to see them."

Sasha slipped the mask string over her head. She surveyed the workshop, looking in all directions while Tucker waited impatiently. "Anything?" he said when he couldn't stand it anymore.

"Just a lot of junk I've seen a bunch of times before," Sasha replied. She took the mask off. "No grelkins."

"Let me try," Tucker said, and Sasha gave him the mask back.

Just like her, he didn't see anything unusual. There wasn't a grelkin in sight. He took the mask off. "I was sure they'd be down here," he said. "Maybe they stayed at school. Or at my house."

"Or maybe they don't really exist," said Sasha.

Tucker glared at her. "They do!" he insisted.

Sasha didn't say anything. Tucker knew she

didn't believe him. Now he was more upset than he had been before. She was probably going to tell all the other kids that he was trying to blame what happened on made-up creatures.

The sound of footsteps on the stairs behind them interrupted Tucker's thoughts. Eke bounded into the room, a look of panic on his face. "You've got to come upstairs!" he said.

"What's going on?" Sasha asked.

Eke shook his head. "I don't even know," he said. "There are leaks *everywhere*. It's like the house has gone crazy. And I *swear* I saw one of your plastic dinosaurs *floating* down the hall."

"It's the grelkins," Tucker said. "It has to be."

"The what?" said Eke. "Those things from the stories?" He looked at his sister. "Is he serious?"

"He is," Sasha said. "I don't know if I believe

him, but we definitely need to go check it out."

Tucker motored his chair over to the elevator, and Sasha shut the door. Tucker pushed the lever up. The elevator rattled and rumbled as it rose to the upper floor. Tucker tapped his fingers impatiently on the arm of his chair. "Come on, come on, come on," he mumbled.

The elevator stopped. Tucker knew it was too soon. He wasn't yet at the top. He jiggled the handle. Nothing happened.

"Thief," a low voice said.

"Scoundrel," said another.

"Brigand," added a third.

In the darkness, Tucker could see nothing. And there was no one to help him.

He did the only thing he could think of to do—he screamed.

9

The grelkins laughed.

Above him, Tucker heard Sasha and Eke pounding on the door to the elevator and calling his name. "Help!" he shouted back. "I'm stuck!"

He fumbled for the lever on the side of the little box. As he did, his hand touched something that moved. A grelkin was hanging from the handle, preventing it from being raised.

Tucker grabbed at the creature, wrapping his hand around its body. The grelkin let out a growl and started beating at him with its fists.

Tucker tossed the grelkin aside, hearing another one grunt as it was knocked over. He gripped the lever firmly and shoved it up. The elevator jerked back to life and ascended. Tucker used his free hand to swat at anything that seemed to be moving around him. Then the elevator was at the top and the door was pulled open. Tucker quickly pressed the bat mask to his face, just in time to see three grelkins running quickly down the hallway. One turned and stuck out its tongue at him.

"They're going that way," Tucker said, pointing after the retreating figures.

Sasha took the mask from him and looked through it. She gasped. "They're real!"

Tucker couldn't resist saying, "I *told* you they were."

"I wonder if they're responsible for all the leaks that are happening," Sasha said.

"We need to go tell Dad," said Eke. "Before the whole house floods."

"Where is he?" Sasha asked.

"Up in the tower," Eke told her.

They went down the hallway toward the elevator that reached the upper floors of the house. As they got in and Eke pushed a button, Sasha turned to Tucker. "The elevator only goes as high as the third floor. We have to climb stairs to get to the tower room."

"You two can do that," Tucker said. "I'll look out for the grelkins."

The elevator stopped, and the three of them exited into another hallway. Water was dripping from a huge wet spot in the ceiling, and a stream of it was trickling toward them. A toy boat floated along as if it were sailing on a river.

"The stairs are at the other end," Sasha said to Tucker. "Wait here."

She and Eke ran down the hall, their feet splashing in the water. Tucker put the bat mask on and scanned for grelkins. He didn't see any. Then he heard giggling coming from one of the rooms. They were nearby. *Hurry up*, he thought, wishing that Sasha and Eke would return with help.

A minute later, they did return. But not with help. They were alone.

"What's the matter?" Tucker asked. "Where are our dads?"

"Locked in the tower room," Sasha said. "Somehow, the grelkins have jammed the lock and we can't get the door open."

"Break it down!" Tucker said.

"Your dad wants us to turn the water off where it comes in the house," Sasha told him. "He says it's easy, and that you'll know what to do because you've helped him lots of times. But we have to go to the basement."

"You mean the workshop?" said Tucker.

Sasha shook her head. "This is in another part of the house."

"Does the elevator go there?" Tucker asked.

Sasha nodded. The three of them got back in the elevator and started to go down.

"Did you tell them about the grelkins?" Tucker asked as they descended.

"No," Sasha admitted. "I figured they're okay as long as they're locked in the tower, and it just sounded so weird."

"It *is* weird," said Tucker. "But I guess I

don't blame you. Nobody wants to believe things like this are actually real."

"I've seen them, and I still don't want to believe they're real," Sasha said.

"Well, I'm not afraid of any stupid grelkins," Eke announced. "We can handle them ourselves."

Sasha, who was standing between the two boys, took one of their hands in each of her own. She squeezed. "You're right," she said as the elevator shuddered to a stop and the doors opened. "We can."

Tucker, who a moment before had been feeling more hopeful, felt a little less so when he saw the basement. It actually looked more like a cave carved out of rock. The walls and floor were stone, and the ceiling was crossed by thick timbers strung with spiderwebs, some of which still had spiders on them. The only light came from bare light bulbs spaced far apart, making small pools of light separated by areas of inky darkness. The air was chilly and damp. He shivered.

"The water pipe should be over there," Sasha said, pointing to one of the corners of the room.

The three of them went in that direction, until they came to a thick steel pipe that protruded from one stone wall. They could hear the sound of water whooshing through it. There was a wheel-like valve handle sticking out of it.

"That's the shutoff," Tucker said. "We just need to turn it off."

Sasha put her hands on the valve handle and tried to turn it. "It's stuck," she said.

Eke put his hands on the other side of the

valve, and together they tried again. This time, there was a rusty squeaking sound and the valve moved a little. The siblings gave another twist, and the sound of running water grew softer. They kept turning, until finally there was no noise at all.

"I think we did it," Sasha said, hugging Eke. "Good teamwork."

"Let's get back upstairs and get our dads out," said Tucker.

They turned and started to go back to the elevator. When they were halfway across the cellar floor, the light bulb above them flickered. Then it went out. So did all the other bulbs. They waited a minute, but nothing came back on.

"It's the grelkins," Sasha said. "They've cut the power off."

"Do you know where the breaker box is?"

Tucker asked. He didn't know exactly what a breaker box was or what it did, but he'd heard his dad mention it once when the power at their house went off.

"No," Sasha said.

It was so dark that Tucker couldn't even see Sasha and Eke, who were right next to him. A second later, a small light appeared. It wasn't big at all, only enough for Tucker to see Sasha and Eke. Eke was holding some kind of action figure in his hand. It had a light in its chest.

"I forgot I had Captain Lightforce in my pocket," Eke said.

It wasn't much, but it was better than being in the dark. Tucker felt himself relax a little bit, at least until Sasha said, "We won't be able to use the elevator."

"Are there stairs?" Tucker asked.

"Yeah," said Sasha. "But they're really narrow. I don't think your chair will fit."

She was right. When they got to the stairs, Tucker discovered that they were a couple of inches too narrow. And even if they had been wide enough, his chair was far too heavy for Sasha and Eke to lift. He was stuck in the cellar.

"You guys go," he said. "I'll wait here."

"One of us will stay with you," Sasha suggested.

Tucker shook his head. "I'll be okay," he said. "And it might take two of you to help get the tower door open. Just hurry."

"At least keep this," Eke said, handing him Captain Lightforce.

"You'll need it to see up there," Tucker said.

"There's a flashlight in the kitchen," Sasha said. "We can make it there even in the dark.

We've done it plenty of times when we've snuck down to get ice cream in the middle of the night."

"Okay," Tucker said, taking the action figure.

"We'll be back as soon as we can," Sasha assured him. Then she and Eke disappeared up the stairs.

Tucker looked around. He didn't think sitting in front of the stairs was the safest place to be, in case something came down them. He wheeled his chair over to the opposite wall and turned it so that his back was to the stones and he was facing the stairs. He put the bat mask on and held the Captain Lightforce figure in his hand. The tiny light coming from it didn't do much, but it made him feel slightly less scared. He hoped Sasha and Eke would get back soon.

A scurrying sound came from his left. He

turned the Captain Lightforce in that direction. A small rat looked back at him, then darted off into the darkness. Tucker wasn't afraid of rats, and he was almost sorry to see it go. "At least you could have kept me company," he called after it.

"Hello, thief," said a voice from the other side of him.

Tucker twisted his body around as much as he could, holding out the Captain Lightforce. At first, there was nothing there. Then the hatless grelkin stepped out of the shadows and into the light. It grinned.

The light on Captain Lightforce's chest started to flicker. *Oh no*, Tucker thought, *the battery is running out.* He shook the toy, as if this might help. The flickering continued, the grelkin appearing and disappearing as the light went on and off. Each time it was revealed, it was a little bit closer.

Tucker gripped the figure, frantically hoping it would stay on. As he squeezed it, a robotic voice said, "Together, we can fight the darkness!"

Tucker hoped Captain Lightforce was right.

10

As the grelkin came closer, Tucker thought about what he might have that could be used to defend himself. The only things in his bag were books, pens, and some candy bars. Then he remembered the grabbing stick. Holding Captain Lightforce in one hand, he felt around for the grabber with the other. His hand closed on it, and he pulled it out. Holding it up like a sword, he cried out, "Don't come any closer!"

The grelkin ignored him, continuing to advance. Tucker poked at it with the grabbing stick, but it dodged him. He worked the handle, opening and closing the prongs at the end of it. The grelkin ducked and kept coming. But then Tucker managed to close the grabber around it. He held it tight. The grelkin fought him, hitting the stick with his hands and letting out a string of very impolite words.

"Unhand me, thief!" it said.

"No," Tucker said. "I'm holding you here until Sasha and Eke get back with our dads."

The grelkin pounded its wooden hands against the grabber and kicked with its feet, but Tucker didn't let go. He scanned the room, looking for signs of the other grelkins, but they seemed to be alone. He guessed the other ones were making mischief somewhere else in the house.

"You're a thief and a scoundrel!" the grelkin shouted.

"I think those are kind of the same thing," Tucker said.

The grelkin muttered something incomprehensible. It thrashed around again. Then it was still. It stared at Tucker. He stared back. The silence made him anxious, so he said the first thing that came to mind. "Did you really set the house on fire because you were mad at Ahab Thatcher?"

"No," the grelkin grunted. "Well, yes. But not on purpose. Thumbfumble left a candle burning and it set some papers on fire."

"Thumbfumble?" said Tucker.

"My brother," the grelkin said. "One of them, anyway. There are a lot. Greasespot, Sootwell, Big Leif and Small Leif, Dave."

"Dave?" Tucker said, laughing despite the fact that he was still pretty scared. "And what's your name?"

The grelkin hesitated. "Redcap," he said. "Because of my red cap."

"But you all have red caps," said Tucker.

"Mine was the best one," Redcap said, crossing his arms over his chest. "And you stole it."

"I did not steal it," Tucker argued. "You lost it and I found it. And it got torn by accident."

The grelkin said nothing.

"You know I'm right," Tucker said. "So why did you do all those nasty things? Everyone thinks I did them."

Redcap shrugged. "We were bored," he said. "It's been a long time since anyone has seen us. Ever since Felix died, there's been nothing to help with in the workshop. We might have gotten a little bit peevish."

"Peevish?" Tucker said.

"It's a synonym for irritable," said Redcap.

Tucker made a note of it. He liked learning new words. "Are you guys making the pipes leak?" he asked.

"Possibly," the grelkin admitted. "That was mostly Dave's idea."

"Can you make it stop?"

Redcap scowled. "Why should we?"

"For one, because this house is really great and you don't want to ruin it. For another, because I didn't steal your cap and you're just doing this because you're angry."

Redcap didn't say anything.

"And three, because I'll get you a new cap," Tucker said. "An even better one."

"Better?" Redcap said. "Better how?"

"You'll just have to wait and see," Tucker said. "Now, can you fix this?"

Redcap looked at him for a long moment. "You'll have to help," he said.

"How?" Tucker asked.

"Put me on your lap," the grelkin instructed.

Now it was Tucker who hesitated. What if Redcap was trying to trick him? He could just wait for Sasha and the others to get there. But he had asked the grelkin to trust him. Maybe he should do the same. He lifted the grabber and brought Redcap closer, opening the claw so that the grelkin dropped gently into his lap.

"Wheel us that way," Redcap said, pointing.

Tucker did, using Captain Lightforce to show the way. When they came to a big metal box on the wall, Redcap pointed to it and said, "Lift me up."

Again, Tucker used the grabber to hoist Redcap into the air. The grelkin opened a door on the box, rummaged around inside, and the lights overhead came back on. Tucker lowered the grelkin back onto his lap, but Redcap jumped down and started walking away. "Come on," he said.

Tucker followed him back to the elevator. With the electricity restored, it worked again, and the two of them rode up to the main floor in silence. Before the doors opened, Redcap said, "I'll go talk to my brothers. There will be no more trouble from us—as long as you keep your promise."

"One new cap," Tucker said. "I'll bring it to you tomorrow after school."

Redcap ran off, leaving Tucker alone in the

hall. A few minutes later, Sasha and Eke came downstairs accompanied by both dads. "How did you get the power back on?" Sasha asked.

"I had some help," Tucker said. "I'll tell you all about it later."

"It's going to take me a while to get all the leaks fixed," Tucker's father said. "But I think it will be okay."

The two dads went off to see what needed to be done, leaving the kids alone again. "Okay," Sasha said. "What happened down there?"

Tucker told her the story.

"And how are you going to make him a new cap?" Sasha asked. "If you don't, he's going to be really angry. I don't want my house burned down or anything."

"Don't you worry," Tucker said. "I've got it covered."

A little while later, he and his dad left, his dad promising to come back the next day to finish up the work that needed to be done. As soon as Tucker got home, he went over to where Great-Aunt Hilda was sitting on the couch, knitting. "I don't suppose you have any red yarn in there, do you?" he asked her.

Great-Aunt Hilda reached into her bag and pulled out a ball of bright red wool. It looked soft and warm. It was perfect. Tucker smiled. "Do you think you can do me a favor?"

———

The next day, when school was over, Tucker asked his mother to drive him over to Sasha's house so they could see how Tucker's dad was getting along with fixing the plumbing. "I think Dr. Okafor is home," Tucker added. "I bet she'd *love* to give you a tour."

He was right about both things. As their mothers went to explore the house, Tucker, Sasha, and Eke went down to the workshop. Tucker put the bat mask on. "Redcap?" he called out. "Big Leif? Little Leif? Dave?"

Grelkins appeared everywhere. Redcap walked across one of the workbenches and stood in front of Tucker and the others.

"Hey," Eke said, "how come we can see you now?"

Tucker took the mask off and placed it on the workbench. He too could still see the grelkins.

"We don't *have* to be invisible," Redcap said. "It's just more fun that way." He looked at Tucker. "Did you bring me a new cap?"

Tucker reached into his bag and brought out the little hat that Great-Aunt Hilda had knitted for him. He handed it to Redcap, who ran his hands over it. "Soft," he said. He put it on his head. "How does it look?"

"Marvelous," said a grelkin that might have been Little Leif.

"Splendid," said another.

"*Cap*ital," said a third, and the rest groaned, "Dave!"

Redcap held out his hand to Tucker. Tucker took it between three fingers and shook. "No more mischief?" he said.

"Maybe just a little?" Redcap replied. "Every third Thursday?"

Tucker looked at Sasha and Eke. They nodded.

"Deal," Tucker said.

The grelkins disappeared back under the workbenches and into the secret hiding places of the workshop. Tucker found himself a little bit disappointed to see them go. But maybe he would be able to come back and see them sometimes.

"What are you going to do with the mask now?" Eke asked him.

Tucker hadn't thought about it. He looked around for the mask. It wasn't where he'd put it on the workbench. He checked his bag, in case he had somehow moved it there, but it wasn't there either. "I think one of the grelkins took it," he said.

From somewhere in the workshop, laughter rippled out. Tucker, Sasha, and Eke laughed back.

"Thief!" Tucker called out.

"Scoundrel!" Sasha said.

"Burglar!" said Eke.

Then they went upstairs to see if there were any cookies in the kitchen.